For Sue Lubeck, who couldn't wait
M.H.

For Taj and all the Mahals:
"Families are what you make them."
C.B.

ISBN 0-590-12243-6

Text copyright © 1995 by Mary Hoffman. Illustrations copyright © 1995 by Caroline Binch. All rights reserved. Published by Scholastic Inc., 555 Broadway, New York, NY 10012, by arrangement with Dial Books for Young Readers, a division of Penguin Books USA Inc. SCHOLASTIC and associated logos are trademarks and/or registered trademarks of Scholastic Inc.

12 11 10 9 8 7 6 5 4 3 2 1   7 8 9/9 0 1 2/0

Printed in the U.S.A.   14

First Scholastic printing, October 1997

Boundless Grace

Sequel to *Amazing Grace*

by Mary Hoffman
pictures by Caroline Binch

SCHOLASTIC INC.
New York   Toronto   London   Auckland   Sydney

Grace lived with her ma and her nana and a cat called Paw-Paw. Next to her family, what Grace liked best was stories. Some she knew and some she made up. She was particularly interested in ones about fathers—because she didn't have one.

"You do too have a father," her ma said when she caught Grace talking that way. "I must have told you a hundred times about how we split up, and your papa went back to Africa. He has another family now, but he's still your father, even though he doesn't live with us anymore."

Well, that wasn't Grace's idea of a father! She wanted one like Beauty's, who brought her roses from the Beast's garden in spite of the dangers. Not one she hadn't seen since she was very little and only knew from letters and photographs.

And in her school reading books Grace saw that all the families had a mother and a father, a boy and a girl, and a dog and a cat.

"Our family's not right," she told Nana. "We need a father and a brother and a dog."

"Well," said Nana, "I'm not sure how Paw-Paw would feel about a dog. And what about me? Are there any nanas in your schoolbooks?"

Grace shook her head.

"Do I have to go then?" asked Nana.

"Of course not!" Grace said, hugging her.

Nana hugged her back. "A family with you in it is a real family," she said. "Families are what you make them."

Then one day when Grace got home from school, she saw a letter on the table with a crocodile stamp on it. Grace knew it must be from Papa, but it wasn't Christmas or her birthday.

"Guess what!" Ma said. "Your papa sent the money for two tickets to visit him in Africa for your spring vacation. Nana says she'll go with you if you want. What do you say?"

But Grace was speechless. She had made up so many fathers for herself, she had forgotten what the real one was like.

Grace and Nana left for Africa on a very cold gray day. They arrived in The Gambia in golden sunshine like the hottest summer back home. It had been a long, long trip. Grace barely noticed the strange sights and sounds that greeted her. She was thinking of Papa.

I wonder if Papa will still love me? thought Grace. He has other children now, and in stories it's always the youngest that is the favorite. She held on tightly to Nana.

Outside the airport was a man who looked a little like Papa's photo. He swung Grace up in his arms and held her close. Grace buried her nose in his shirt and thought, I do remember.

In the car she started to notice how different everything seemed. There were sheep wandering along the roadside and people selling watermelons under the trees.

And when they reached her father's compound, there was the biggest difference of all. A pretty young woman with a little girl and a baby boy came to meet them. Grace said hello, but couldn't manage another word all evening. Everyone thought she was just tired. Except Nana.

"What's the matter, honey?" she asked when they went to bed. "You've got a father and a brother now, and they even have a dog!"

But Grace thought, They make a storybook family without me. I'm one girl too many. Besides, it's the wrong Ma.

The next day Grace started to get to know Neneh and
Bakary. The children thought it was wonderful to have
a big sister all the way from America. And Grace couldn't
help liking them too. But she had to feel cross with some-
one. Grace knew lots of stories about wicked stepmothers
—*Cinderella, Snow White, Hansel and Gretel*—so she
decided to be cross with Jatou. I won't clean the house
for her, thought Grace. I won't eat anything she cooks,
and I won't let her take me into the forest.

Jatou made a big dish of
savory benachin for lunch,
but Grace wouldn't eat any.
"I'm not hungry," she said.
    "She's probably still getting
over the long flight," said Jatou.

When Papa came home from work, he found Grace in the backyard. He sat beside her under the big old jackfruit tree. "This is where my grandma used to tell me stories when I was a little boy," he said.

"Nana tells me stories too," said Grace.

"Did she ever tell you the one about how your ma and I came to split up?" asked Papa.

"I know that one," said Grace, "but I don't want to hear it right now," and she covered up her ears.

Papa hugged her. "Would you like the one about the papa who loved his little girl so much, he saved up all his money to bring her to visit him?"

"Yes, I'd like that one," said Grace.

"Okay. But if I tell you that story, will you promise to try to be nice to Jatou? You're both very important to me," said Papa.

Grace thought about it. "I'll try," she said.

The next day they went to the market. It was much more exciting than shopping at home. Even the money had crocodiles on it! Lots of the women carried their shopping on their head.

Then they went to a stall that was like stepping inside a
rainbow. There was cloth with crocodiles and elephants
on it and cloth with patterns made from pebbles and shells.
And so many colors!

"We can choose cloth for Grace's first African dress,"
said Papa. Grace and Nana spent a long time choosing.
No one was in a hurry.

The days of Grace's visit flew by. She played in the
ocean with her brother and sister, and she told them a
bedtime story every night. She told all the stories she
knew—*Beauty and the Beast, Rapunzel, Rumpelstiltskin.*
It was amazing how many stories were about fathers who
gave their daughters away. But she didn't tell them any
about wicked stepmothers.

Sometimes Ma called from home and her voice made Grace feel homesick. "I feel like gum, stretched out all thin in a bubble," she told Nana. "As if there isn't enough of me to go around. I can't manage two families. What if I burst?"

"Seems to me there *is* enough of you, Grace," said Nana. "Plenty to go around. And remember, families are what you make them."

Soon it was their last evening and there was a big
farewell party at the compound. Grace and Nana wore
their African clothes and Grace ate twice as much
benachin as everyone else. "Now you really might burst,"
said Nana.

On their last morning Papa took Grace to see some real crocodiles. "This is a special holy place," he said. "The crocodiles are so tame, you can stroke them."

"Not like the one in *Peter Pan*!" said Grace.

"No. These are so special, you can make a wish on them," said Papa.

Grace closed her eyes and made a wish, but she
wouldn't say what it was.

Later at the compound Grace asked Nana, "Why aren't there any stories about families like mine, that don't live together?"

"Well, at least you've stopped thinking it's your family that's wrong," said Nana. "Now, until we get back home and find some books about families like yours, you'll just have to make up a new story of your own."

"I'll do that," said Grace, "and when we're home again, I'll write it down and send it to Jatou to read to Neneh and Bakary."

The whole family came to see them off at the airport. Grace was sorry to say good-bye to her new brother and sister and even to her stepmother. But leaving Papa was hardest of all.

Waiting for their plane, Nana asked Grace if she had thought anymore about her story.

"Yes, but I can't think of the right ending," said Grace, "because the story's still going on."

"How about they lived happily ever after?" asked Nana.

"That's a good one," said Grace. "Or they lived happily ever after, though not all in the same place?"

"Stories are what you make them," said Nana.

"Just like families," said Grace.